T0132099

ABOVE THE WORLD, SO HIGH

SO HIGH

WRITTEN AND ILLUSTRATED BY

PENELOPE BEACH CHITTENDEN

Copyright © 2021 by PENELOPE BEACH CHITTENDEN. 832974

All rights reserved. No part of this book may be reproduced
or transmitted in any form or by any means, electronic or
mechanical, including photocopying, recording, or by any
information storage and retrieval system, without permission in
writing from the copyright owner.

This is a work of fiction. Names, characters, places and
incidents either are the product of the author's imagination
or are used fictitiously, and any resemblance to any actual
persons, living or dead, events, or locales is entirely
coincidental.

To order additional copies of this book, contact:
Xlibris
844-714-8691
www.Xlibris.com
Orders@Xlibris.com

ISBN: 978-1-6641-0991-9 (sc)
ISBN: 978-1-6641-0993-3 (hc)
ISBN: 978-1-6641-0992-6 (e)

Print information available on the last page

Rev. date: 10/06/2021

ABOVE THE WORLD, SO HIGH

Once upon a time before stars filled the sky, a lonely lion roamed the world looking for a friend. Leo was an old lion, too old to go hunting with the young lions Small animals were afraid of him. He wanted to find someone to play with.

So, in that long ago time when animals could talk and horses could fly, Leo climbed to the highest point in the world. From there he could see all the land and oceans

He saw a bull and a horse
grazing in a meadow

Leo spied a white goat clinging to a mountain crag.

He saw a big brown bear fishing in a rushing river.

On a distant hillside a little black bear was munching berries.

Squinting into the sunlight, Leo could see a scorpion sleeping in a vast sandy desert.

Slowly turning his mighty head, Leo surveyed the valleys and peaks. Beyond a great ocean, high on a cliff stood a big ram with large horns.

Leo opened his very large mouth and roared.

HELLOOOO

The brown bear growled a deep

HELLO OOOOOO

The ram B

       A

          A-ed

The goat *MAAA -ed*

The bull snorted. The horse kept on grazing, because he did not want to say "neigh".

The scorpion wagged his stinging tail.

And little black bear growled a small *HELLOO*

They made so much noise that a crab sunning herself at the edge of tidal pool heard the noise. She quickly scurried off to tell her friend Pisces, the fish to swim up to the top of the ocean to listen.

Leo roared again, "Will you be my friends?"

The big bull nodded. Big bear growled, "Yes".

Little black bear asked, "Will you eat me.?

"Of course I won't eat you. Friends don't eat friends", answered Leo.

Crab and Pisces just listened.

"You are far away. Where can we play?" asked the ram.

"In the sky," answered Leo. "We can play in the sky."

Just then they all heard a loud flapping sound. WHOOSH, Aquila, the eagle darted into the air. "The sky is mine, all mine. I live alone in the sky," screeched Aquila

Little bear watched. "All alone?, poor bird, I will be your friend," he said.

The eagle soared happily into the air again. "A friend, I have a friend! But how can you fly up to the sky? You have no wings."

The animals did not know how they could fly to the sky, except the horse who had wings.

Then they, blew bubbles, lots and lots of bubbles.

Bubbles floated all
over the world.

"Ride up on the bubbles," shouted Aquila. Crab
and Pisces blew more and more bubbles.

Up floated big brown bear
and little black bear.

Up floated Taurus the bull. Pegasus, the horse, spread his wings and flew.

Crab and Pisces blew two huge bubbles for Leo to ride on. "Come with us", he called to the bubble blowers.

The ram and the goat rode up with the scorpion right behind.

So crab and the fish floated on their own bubbles to join their friends high in the sky.

And there they played until the bubbles burst into a billion shards of glistening light. Some stars stuck to them and that is why you can see the animals in the night sky.

GOODNIGHT

SCORPIO

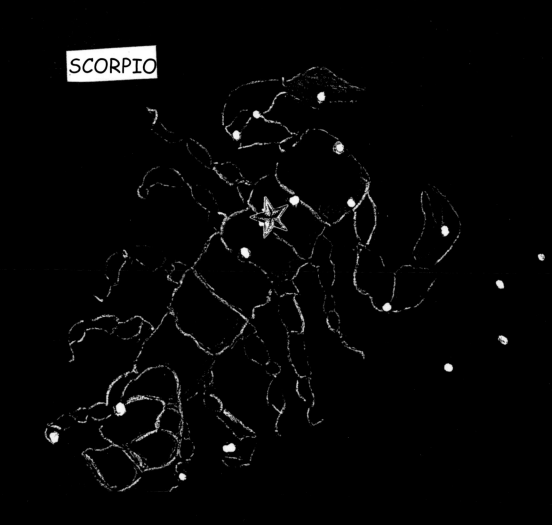

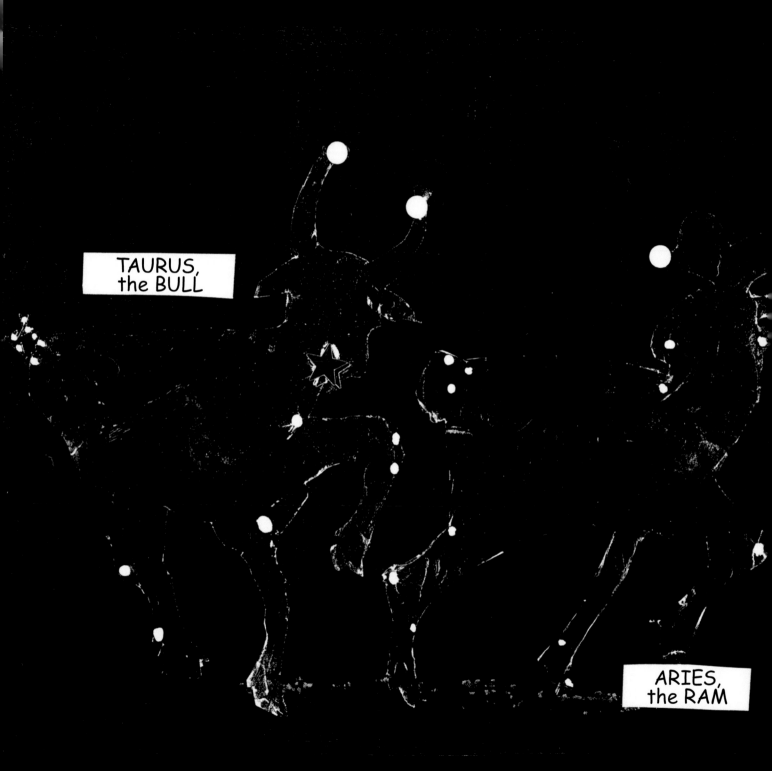

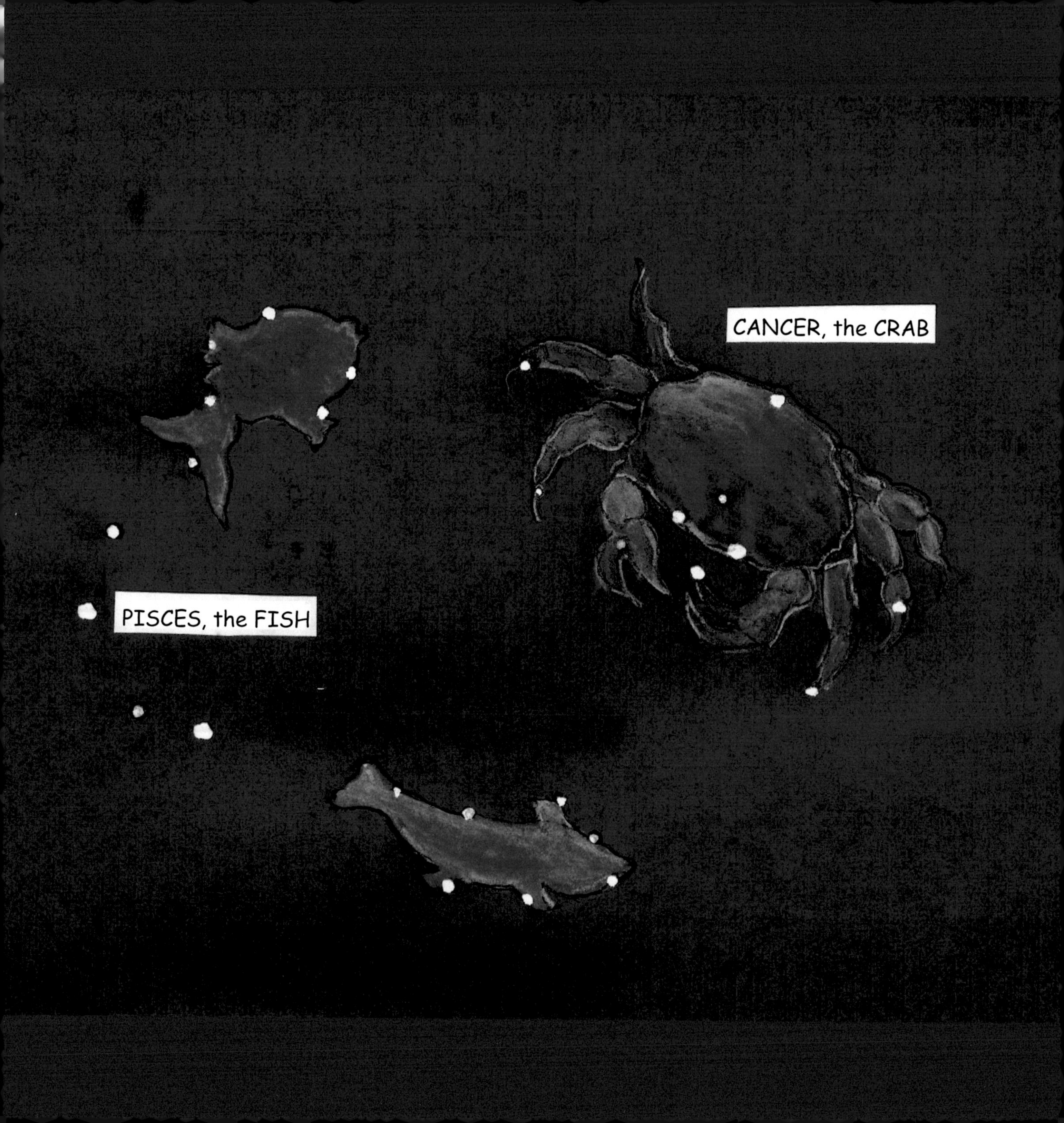
CANCER, the CRAB
PISCES, the FISH

CAPRICORN: a horned goat, although small and faint, is the 10th sign of the Zodiac, The zodiac is like a belt, composed of 12 constellations, around the sky. Our sun travels across the zodiac in its annual journey.

LEO: The 5th sign of the Zodiac, represents the lion that the Greek hero, Hercules, strangled and killed. The very bright star in Leo's paw is named Regulus. Look in a straight line from Polaris, the North Star, downward through two stars of the Big Dipper to the ???

Long, long ago, before television, the sky was the big screen on which 'moving stars' acted out stories that ancient man made up. The brightest of the stars were given names, such as Antares in the constellation of Scorpio, Regulus in Leo, and Altair in Aquila. As time went by more animals joined the sky dwellers, including a dog. The brightest star in the sky is Sirius in the dog constellation. The stars are very important to travelers and to sailors. By locating the North Star at the tail of the Little Bear, they will know where they are going. So twinkle, twinkle, every star . . . .

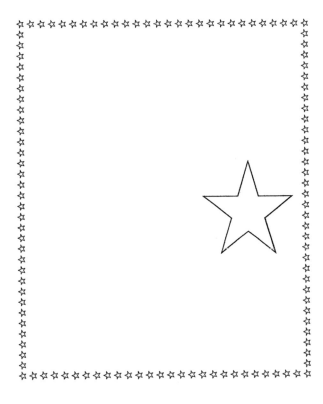

"When other animals saw how much fun Leo and the bears and fish were having they joined them in the sky. Lepus the hare, Cetus the whale and Camelopardis followed Cygnus the swan and the 2 dogs up to the sky."

LEO: The 5th sign of the Zodiac, during the summer represents the lion that the Greek hero, Hercules, strangled and killed. The very bright star in Leo's paw is named Regulus. Look in a straight line from Polaris, the North Star, down through two stars of the Big Dipper to the next bright star. That is Regulus, in Leo's paw.

CAPRICORN: a horned goat, although small and faint, is the 10th sign of the Zodiac, The zodiac is like a belt, composed of 12 constellations, around the sky. Our sun travels across the zodiac in its annual journey.

PISCES: In the 12th constellation in the Zodiac, two fishes are hooked by two lines joined at the end. They represent Venus and Cupid, who, in a Greek myth, disguised themselves to escape a terrible giant..

URSA MAJOR: The big bear is best identified by the Big Dipper, 7 of the 18 easily visible stars in this large constellation.

URSA MINOR: The little bear is best know for Polaris, the north star, which you can find by following a straight line north from the 2 'pointer stars' in the Big Dipper. The North Star is a compass guide for sailors and travelers.

CANCER: The crab is a small group of faint stars, important only because it is the 4th sign of the Zodiac.

SCORPIO: This long beautiful constellation lies near the horizon in the southern sky. Its brightest star, Antares, is a supergiant 3000 times brighter than our sun. In mythology the scorpion killed the hunter Orion.

TAURUS: The most identifiable part of the Bull constellation is the cluster of stars at the end of one horn known as the Pleiades, or the 7 Sisters. The brightest star in this 2nd sign of the zodiac is Aldebaran.

PEGASUS: The winged horse flies across the late summer sky. His wings form a bright triangle of stars. These three stars plus one in the nearby constellation of Andromeda form a large rectangle. Look for it half way between the North Star and the horizon.

AQUILA: The eagle, with wings spread, can be seen in summer. Altair, a star of the first magnitude, is one of the brightest stars in our sky.

ARIES: The sun passes through this 1st sign of the zodiac in March but can best be seen in winter. In Greek mythology Aries was the Ram with the Golden Fleece that Jason sought.

Printed in the United States
by Baker & Taylor Publisher Services